Jacqueline and the Beanstalk

For Krista, brave facer of fears—SDS
For Nadia, fun, feisty, fearless—BSM

To the brave Helena!—VD

Published by
MAGINATION PRESS ®
An Educational Publishing Foundation Book
American Psychological Association
750 First Street NE
Washington, DC 20002

Magination Press is a registered trademark of the American Psychological Association.

For more information about our books, including a complete catalog, please write to us, call 1-800-374-2721, or visit our website at www.apa.org/pubs/magination.

Book design by Susan K. White
Printed by Lake Book Manufacturing, Inc., Melrose Park, IL

Library of Congress Cataloging-in-Publication Data
Names: Sweet, Susan D., author. | Miles, Brenda, author. |
    Docampo, Valeria, 1976- illustrator.
Title: Jacqueline and the beanstalk : a tale of facing giant fears /
    by Susan D. Sweet, PhD, and Brenda S. Miles, PhD ; illustrated by Valeria Docampo.
Description: Washington, DC : Magination Press, [2017] |
    "American Psychological Association." | Summary: An overprotected princess
    convinces the knights who guard her and the giant who lives above them not to be
    afraid of one another.
Identifiers: LCCN 2016031999| ISBN 9781433826825 (hardcover) |
    ISBN 1433826828 (hardcover)
Subjects: | CYAC: Fear—Fiction. | Princesses—Fiction. |
    Knights and Knighthood—Fiction. | Giants—Fiction.
Classification: LCC PZ7.1.S93 Be 2017 | DDC [E]—dc23 LC record available at
    https://lccn.loc.gov/2016031999

Manufactured in the United States of America
10 9 8 7 6 5 4 3 2 1

Jacqueline and the Beanstalk

A Tale of Facing Giant Fears

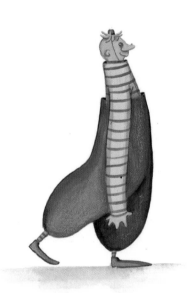

by Susan D. Sweet, PhD
and Brenda S. Miles, PhD

illustrated by Valeria Docampo

MAGINATION PRESS · WASHINGTON, DC
American Psychological Association

Once upon a time there lived a princess
named Jacqueline. The royal knights protected her—
from EVERYTHING!

"Shields up! There mighteth be danger!"

"But there might not be," said the princess,
"and I can't see!"

"Shields up! There mighteth be danger!"

"But there might not be," said the princess, "and I can't twirl!"

"Shields up! There mighteth be danger!"

"But there might not be,"
said the princess,
"and I can't reach!"

The knights worried most when Jacqueline walked by the beanstalk.

"Helloooo, Mr. Giant!" she called.

"Shhhh! He might heareth," said a knight.

"He's nasty," said another.
"My tummy hurteth just thinking about him."

"But you've never climbed up to meet him,"
said Jacqueline. "What if he's nice?"

"Nuh uh! He's different, and different meaneth danger."

"We'll never know if we don't go," the princess insisted.

"Hark, no! We won't go!"

"Suit yourselves," said the princess.

Later, when midnight chimed,
the princess climbed.
And at the top…

"AHHHH! Human! Different! Danger!"

"Me? Dangerous? I'm the size of your toenail!"

"True," said the giant, "but your kingdom is dangerous!"

"You've never climbed down to meet us. We're actually quite nice," said the princess. "You'll never know if you don't go!"

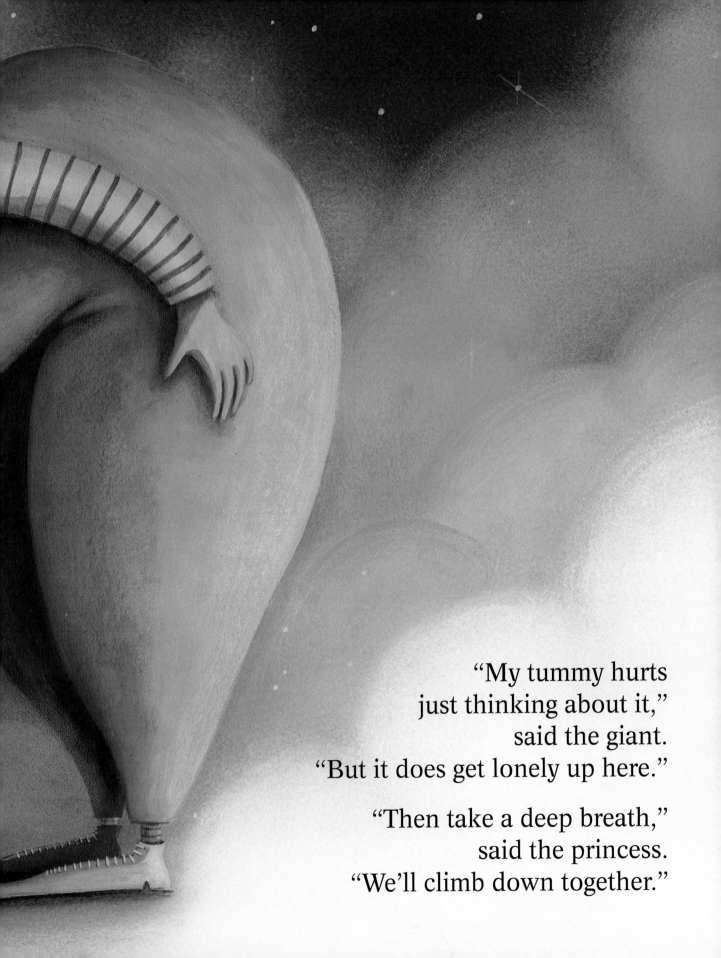

"My tummy hurts
just thinking about it,"
said the giant.
"But it does get lonely up here."

"Then take a deep breath,"
said the princess.
"We'll climb down together."

And so they did—one step at a time.

"Helloooo, royal knights," Jacqueline called
as the kingdom came closer.

"Shields up! Protecteth the princess! Wait!
Where is the princess?"

"I'm up here, and there's nothing to fear!"

But at the bottom…

"AHHHH! Knights! Swords! Poking!"

"AHHHH! Giant! Stepping! Squashing!"

"Wait!" said the princess.
"No one's going to poke or squash anyone!"

"Maybe you're righteth..." said the knights.
"Shields down."

"I guess..." said the giant. "Feet down."

Feeling less worried took some time,
but then the whole kingdom started to climb!

Soon everyone learned that different wasn't dangerous. It was delightful!

And forever after, the princess never missed a thing.
In fact, she had the best view of all!

Note to Parents and Caregivers

"Worry often gives a small thing a big shadow." — Swedish proverb

The knights of the kingdom see danger everywhere. Maybe your child does, too. Does your child:

- Think of twenty things that *might* go wrong before the day has even started?
- Lie awake at night worrying about "what ifs"?
- Complain of stomachaches or headaches that seem to pop up when challenges appear?
- Sometimes miss out because trying something new feels too scary?

If your child struggles with worries, he or she is not alone. Anxiety is the most common mental health concern among children and youth—and among adults, too! It can be difficult to know what to do, but there are tools that can help, and childhood is a great time to start learning them!

What Happens When We Worry?

Our bodies. When faced with danger, our bodies have a built-in alarm system that gets us ready to react. It's called the "fight-flight-freeze" response. We may sweat or experience stomachaches or headaches. We may feel flushed, shaky, dizzy, hot or cold, or we may experience other sensations. Everyone's alarm system is different, and some alarms go off more easily than others. Some even go off when there is no real danger! But the physical sensations are just as uncomfortable.

Our feelings. In addition to worry, sometimes we also experience other feelings, like loneliness, frustration, or sadness.

Our thoughts. Most thoughts revolve around anticipatory worry—worry about the future and what *might* go wrong. Children who worry are fantastic at "what ifs." *What if people laugh at me? What if I don't know what to do?* These thoughts can be very hard to shut off, even for adults.

Our behaviors. When most of us feel worried, our first instinct is to stay away from whatever scares us. It feels good in the short term, but in the long term it can make worry worse. Avoidance prevents us from learning that things might not be as bad as we think, and from seeing whether or not we can actually cope with what we fear. Children who worry may also seek repeated reassurance. *Are you sure you'll pick me up on time? Are you sure nothing bad will happen?* And answering, "Yes, I'm sure," doesn't always seem to help.

Managing Worries

So how can we manage worries? Did you notice we used the word "manage"? That's because humans are wired to experience worry, so aiming for zero just isn't realistic. But keeping worry to a level where it doesn't get in the way of everyday life is *very* realistic.

Here are some strategies to try. Keep as many of them as possible in your worry-busting backpack so you'll be ready to help your child when worries arise!

Explain that everyone worries. Let your child know that worries happen to everyone at times. Discuss what worries your child. Take the time to listen and accept your child's fears as real, even if they seem unrealistic to you.

Examine body cues. Help your child figure out body cues that signal worry. Draw an outline of your child's body and map what happens when worry starts. Does your child's heart beat fast?

Is his or her tummy full of butterflies? Knowing these signs can be helpful because they tell your child it's time to start using coping strategies. Understanding body cues can also help your child learn the difference between feeling sick and feeling worried.

Calm physical sensations. Practice ways to calm the physical side of worry. *Exercise* is a great tool. When our bodies feel keyed up, doing something that matches that physical feeling—like running or jumping or riding a bike—can help our bodies calm down when we stop the activity. When we feel anxious we tend to breathe quickly. Taking *slow, deep breaths* in through the nose and out through the mouth can also help calm our bodies down. Try breathing in, holding, breathing out, and holding again while counting to three on each step. Or try blowing soap bubbles or bubbles in water through a straw. Another way to calm our bodies is through *muscle relaxation*. Tensing and relaxing our muscles can help undo the knots. Squeeze your hands like you are making orange juice and then let them relax. Or try to touch your ears with your shoulders and then lower them again. There are many guided scripts for breathing and muscle relaxation available in apps for mobile devices and on the Internet. *Practicing when you are calm* helps you be ready to use these strategies when you are not so calm, so introduce them when your child's worries are nowhere in sight!

Shift attention. *Distraction* can be a powerful tool. When we are doing something that takes most of our attention, we don't have much left for worrying! Think about what works best for your child. Is it reading, music, or drawing? Is it a great movie or video game, or a walk through the park with a friend?

Work on problem solving. Try turning "what ifs?" into "what thens?" So *what if* that happens? What could you do *then*? Help your child think of options, choose the one that seems best, try it out,

and reflect on how well it worked.

Think differently. Practice helpful thoughts. Ask your child, "What do you think will happen or go wrong?" and then develop a helpful thought that fits the worry. Younger children may have some trouble telling you what they are thinking, but they can still practice helpful thoughts. These thoughts aren't about everything turning out perfectly. They are just more balanced and realistic than worried thinking tends to be. Here are some examples of helpful thoughts:

- "All I can do is try my best."
- "I won't know if I don't try."
- "It won't last forever."

Face fears. Once your child has developed some skills to cope with worries, it's time to *face fears*. This involves exposure—facing what you are afraid of (as long as no real danger is present) over and over until you aren't so afraid. *Exposure* can be a difficult concept for children to understand, but it absolutely works! Make a list of your child's worries and try ordering them from the smallest to the biggest. Then move through the list, one worry at a time, starting with the least scary. Practice facing each fear while your child uses coping strategies until the worry doesn't seem so big anymore. Go slowly, and be patient. Let your child help set the pace. Encourage, support, and praise your child. Remember, it's not easy for any of us to face our fears!

Avoid giving excessive reassurance. Being overly protective or excessively reassuring implies that there is something to be protected from. Give the message that you believe your child can cope. Encourage coping

whenever possible—with the strategies you've learned together—and try not to rearrange your family's life around your child's fears.

Model coping when you can. The next time you feel worried, talk out loud as you try to manage your own fears so your child can see how it's done.

Reduce other stresses. Try to ensure that your home is a predictable place where your child knows what to expect, and what is expected. Predictability can help free up some of your child's energy to use on other things.

Take care of yourself. Parenting a worried child can be challenging. Be kind to yourself, and take a break when you need to.

Seek support. While some worry can be a good thing, worry that grows so big that it interferes with life can be a problem. Worry that causes significant distress or that seems bigger than expected for your child's age and developmental stage likely requires additional help. Seek the support of a licensed professional, such as your family doctor or a psychologist or psychiatrist, if worry is getting in the way.

About the Authors

SUSAN D. SWEET, PHD, is a clinical child psychologist and mother of two. She has worked in hospital, school, and community-based settings and is passionate about children's mental health and well-being. Susan hopes worries never overshadow anyone's dreams.

BRENDA S. MILES, PHD, is a pediatric neuropsychologist who has worked in hospital, rehabilitation, and school settings. Brenda has conquered her fear of writing, despite the risk of rejections, revisions, and writer's block. As for her other fears, she's still working on them!

Susan and Brenda have also co-authored *Princess Penelopea Hates Peas: A Tale of Picky Eating and Avoiding Catastropeas, King Calm: Mindful Gorilla in the City, Cinderstella: A Tale of Planets Not Princes,* and *Chicken or Egg: Who Comes First?*

About the Illustrator

VALERIA DOCAMPO'S inspiration for her art is rooted in everyday life: the eyes of a dog, the shape of a tree, the sound of rainfall, and the aromas of breakfast. Born in Buenos Aires, Argentina, she studied fine arts and graphic design at the University of Buenos Aires. She has illustrated several books for children, notably *The Nutcracker* for the New York City Ballet, *Tout au Bord, Phileas's Fortune,* and *Not Every Princess.*

About Magination Press

MAGINATION PRESS is an imprint of the American Psychological Association, the largest scientific and professional organization representing psychologists in the United States and the largest association of psychologists worldwide.